William Cowper, Thomas Wright

The Unpublished and Uncollected Poems

William Cowper, Thomas Wright

The Unpublished and Uncollected Poems

ISBN/EAN: 9783337123864

Printed in Europe, USA, Canada, Australia, Japan

Cover: Foto ©Andreas Hilbeck / pixelio.de

More available books at **www.hansebooks.com**

The Unpublished
and
Uncollected Poems
of William Cowper

Edited by

THOMAS WRIGHT,

Principal of Cowper School, Olney, and
Author of "The Life of William Cowper," &c.

CAMEO SERIES

T. Fisher Unwin PaternosterSq.
London E.C. MDCCCC.

Contents.

7

List of Illustrations.

Introduction.

THIS volume contains twenty-seven poems, fragments, or couplets. Of these, some have never been published, some have been published only in part, some are passages which for various reasons, and not necessarily on account of their inferiority, were cancelled by Cowper, and some have appeared only in periodicals not now easily accessible, as for example *The Universal Review* (June, 1890). Particulars will be found at the end of each poem.

It is not pretended that these pieces will add anything to Cowper's reputation, though the lines entitled "A Song of Mercy and Judgment" certainly contain some fine stanzas, and the poem on Keppel is not lacking in either feeling or eloquence.

At a time when the sovereign is almost worshipped it is pleasant to read such a production as that "On Loyalty"; and "Box and Bays" though only a morsel, illustrates a very charming feature in Cowper's character—his love for children. The brilliant gem "To Mary" is here exhibited with a new facet.

The Presentation of Cowper's House— now the Cowper Museum—at Olney, to the Town and Nation by W. H. Collingridge, Esq., on the centenary of the Poet's death, is a very notable event in the history of English Literature; but Mr. Collingridge, piling Ossa upon Pelion, presented at the same time his Cowper Collection, including the valuable MS. of the lines on Yardley Oak—which, consequently is now easily consultable. This poem, in order that students may be able to note the principal alterations made by Cowper, is here given in its entirety with the excised passages restored.

The reader will notice the graphic allusion to the good fortune of our great forefather Adam, who

> " was excused the penalties of dull
> Minority ; no primer with his thumb
> He soiled, no grammar with his tears."

It is singular that Cowper—striking out these clear-cut and arresting words—should have substituted the faint and unrememberable :

> " No tutor charged his hand
> With the thought-tracing quill, or tasked his mind
> With problems !"

The poem, however, was left unfinished.

For the convenience of the public I have also printed the whole of the poem " To Mary " with the variants, and the published version of " The Bee and the Pineapple," here entitled "Another on the Same," as well as the less familiar version. Finally I have included a few couplets and other morsels which, though entirely devoid of literary merit, illustrate Cowper's funny habit of dropping at all times and on any occasion into playful rhyme.

My thanks are due to E. P. Ash, Esq., of Haileybury College, for the use of the manuscripts so kindly lent by him to the Cowper Museum, and to F. Barker, Esq., 41, Gunterstone Road, West Kensington, for the poem " On Loyalty."

On the day that Cowper's House passed to the town of Olney, was founded the Cowper Society, to the members of which I have the pleasure of dedicating this volume.

THOMAS WRIGHT.

COWPER SCHOOL, OLNEY,
    July 2, 1900.

THE COWPER MUSEUM

(Cowper's House, Olney).

On Loyalty.

A POEM IN LATIN SENT TO " DEAR TOBY "
(PROBABLY MR. CLOTWORTHY ROWLEY)
IN 1754.

The only introduction Cowper gives is the following :—

" I HAVE twisted the sense of the words
to your present condition as much as
possible ; not taking Horace's meaning,
which I suppose you would choose."

No doubt the passage he refers to is the well-known
line in Epistle II. to Lollius :—

Quicquid delirant reges, plectuntur Achivi
(When kings make fools of themselves the people
    suffer),

which is certainly the opposite sentiment to that in
Cowper's verses.

The following is Cowper's poem :—

Cumtot sustineant Reges et tanta, neque ulla
    Parte, voluptati Deliciisque vacent :
Cum varios capiti affigat Diadema Dolores,
    Bellorumque premant sollicitentque Minae:
Curqueritur Populus ? cur caeco murmure
    mussat ?
    Inque suum Insane vim meditatur Herum ?
Qui Vigil excubias agit usque et (sustinet)
    usque
    Imperii, Populus nequa Laboret, onus.
Hoc Satanæ scelus est nec Dæmone dignius
    ul(lum)
    Nam primum in Satanæ pectore crime(n
    erat)
Præmia quin date digna viro verusque
    sequatur
    Collata in gentem commoda gentis amor.
Illum Jure colant Populi, tueantur, amante(s);
    Ille colit Populos, ille tuetur amat.

Tu vero (si talis erit) quicunque verendum
  Execrare caput Principis, Eia ! Tace,
Necquia rara, fides Regi fert præmia, Demens
  Immeritum Regem quem venerere, putes ;
Ipse tibi plaudas, quae laus est optima,
    Laudem
  Externam Ingenuis est meruisse satis.

The following translation has been written for me
by the Rev. J. Tarver, M.A., Rector of Filgrave,
Bucks :—

Since kings sustain the burdens of the state,
No pleasant hours, no leisure for the great.
Since the uneasy head which wears a crown
The threatenings of impending wars weigh
    down,
Why do the people rage with murmurs dark
Ready to fall on him who steers the bark ?
'Tis his to watch, attent to every call
Lest any burden on his people fall.
'Tis Satan leads astray with devilish art
For Satan ever takes the fouler part.
Nay, rather, be the people's love his due
Who to his people's love is always true,
Him let the nations love and guard and bless,

Whom, loving, guarding, blessing, all confess.
But thou, if such thou art, who dar'st with ill
To curse that sacred head—Oh, " Peace be
    still."
Truth to the king may meet with rare reward,
Think not his claim on thee is therefore
    barred,
Approve thyself praiseworthy—that is best,
Only deserving, loyal souls can rest.

The above poem has never been printed except
privately.

A Song of Mercy and Judgment.[1]

WRITTEN AT ST. ALBANS IN 1764, AFTER THE POET'S RECOVERY.

I.

LORD, I love the habitation
    Where the Saviour's honour dwells.
At the sound of Thy salvation
    With delight my bosom swells.
        Grace Divine, how sweet the sound,
        Sweet the grace that I have found.

II.

Me thro' waves of deep affliction,
    Dearest Saviour ! Thou hast brought,

[1] Compare the peacefulness and serenity of these lines with the *sturm und drang* of the awful sapphics, " Hatred and Vengeance," written just before the derangement. Dr. Cotton, under God, had indeed worked wonders.

Fiery deeps of sharp conviction
  Hard to bear and passing thought.
    Sweet the sound of grace Divine,
    Sweet the grace which makes me Thine.

III.

From the cheerful Beams of morning
  Sad I turned mine eyes away :
And the shades of night returning
  Filled my soul with new dismay.
    Grace Divine, &c.

IV.

Food I loathed, nor ever tasted
  But by violence constrained.
Strength decay'd and body wasted
  Spoke the terrors I sustained.
    Sweet the sound, &c.

V.

Bound and watch'd, lest Life abhorring,
  I should my own death procure,
For to me the Pit of Roaring
  Seem'd more easy to endure.
    Grace Divine, &c.

VI.

Fear of Thee, with gloomy sadness,
  Overwhelm'd Thy guilty worm,
Till reduced to moping madness,
  Reason sank beneath the storm.
    Sweet the sound, &c.

VII.

Then, what soul-distressing noises
  Seemed to reach me from below,
Visionary scenes and voices,
  Flames of Hell, and screams of woe ! [1]
    Grace Divine, &c.

VIII.

But at length a word of Healing,
  Sweeter than an angel's note,
From the Saviour's lips distilling,
  Chas'd despair and chang'd my lot.
    Sweet the sound, &c.

[1] Voices, sometimes consoling, but more frequently terrorising were heard, or seemed to be heard by Cowper, all through his life. Perhaps no clair-audient ever left so minute an account of his experiences as Cowper. See the very original and intensely interesting series of articles entitled " Clair-audience " in the *General Practitioner*, by Dr. Barker Smith ; and my " Life of William Cowper," pages 585-594.

IX.

'Twas a word well-timed and suited
  To the need of such an hour,
Sweet to one like me polluted,
  Spoke in love and sealed with power.

X.

" I," He said, " have seen thee grieving,
  Lov'd thee as I passed thee by.
Be not faithless, but Believing,
  Look and live and never die.

XI.

" Take the bloody seal I give thee,
  Deep impressed upon thy soul ;
God, thy God will now receive thee,
  Faith hath sav'd thee, thou art whole."
    Grace Divine, &c.

XII.

All at once, my chains were broken,
  From my feet my fetters fell,
And that word, in pity spoken,
  Snatched me from the gates of Hell.
    Grace Divine, &c.

XIII.

Since that hour, in hope of glory,
  With Thy foll'wers I am found,
And relate the wond'rous story
  To Thy list'ning saints around.
      Sweet the sound of grace Divine,
      Sweet the grace which makes me Thine.

This poem has appeared only in *The Universal Review*.

A Thunder Storm.

A crude off-hand production written (probably about 1768) at Warrington Lodge, near Olney, whilst Cowper was taking shelter from a storm. Given to me by the late Rev. William Barker, of Hastings. It has appeared only in my "Life of William Cowper."

THE Sky begins to lower and thickening
　　Clouds
Portend a speedy storm, the Vocal tribes
No longer Sonnets sing ; all, *all* are mute ;
The Beasts forbear to graze and seek the
　　shade´:
Yon herd of Swine see, see how fast they
　　run ;
'Tis said they see the Wind—

A solemn and awful silence now prevails,
Save when the breeze the Thunder's har-
    binger
Just rustles through the Grove : on ev'ry
    brow
A dark despondence reigns, and hark ! it
    comes ;
I heard the sudden roar,—my Soul, be calm,
Look up and view its progress, be serene,
Calm and collected, as becomes a Man.
Again it roars—and now the Lightning flies ;
Not faster flies the timid Hare from Hounds ;
Nor from the Victor flies the vanquished Foe,
Than Travellers seek for Shelter, e'en my
    Dog
Cow'rs at my feet and looks up for protec-
    tion,
And now 'tis dreadful truly—Heav'n and
    Earth
How hard it rains ! the Atmosphere's on
    fire !
Chaos presides ! Confusion quite surrounds
    me !
Yet, yet again the broad expanded glare
Of vivid Lightning flashes o'er the Plain

Leaving a sulph'rous stench; Heav'ns what
  a Peal!
Still; still it roars incessant! What to this
The din of armies on the hostile Plain?
An Atom to a Mountain.—
See the sky opens—shuts—and forky fires
Dart oblique to the Earth; and o'er my
  Head
Tempest rides forward on the Whirlwind's
  wing:
Still the Almighty flashes for his Spear;
His Chariot wheels most awfully resound:
Well! be it so my Soul, consoling thought!
He is thy maker and I trust thy friend;
Then wherefore tremble, wherefore shudder
  thus?
No, I will cease to fear, tho' even now
The Ear of Nature feels so strong a Shock
As scarce before it felt: Yet as a Man,
A Christian Man, I shudder now no more.
When God in Thunder spoke from Sinai's
  mount,
Israel approached with Awe, if Moses then
Could mediate for the People, and avert
The great Jehovah's anger, sure his Son,

The fam'd Immanuel, the Prince of Peace,
Can ransom from his wrath and reconcile.
  But oh ! my Soul how poor a Portrait
    this !
How weak the Colours and how faint th'
    Idea,
Of what one day thou must be a Spectator !
Oh ! bright and blessed morning to the Just !
Oh ! Day of doom of infinite distress ;
To those who unprepar'd Messiah meet ;
When thron'd in Clouds, surrounded by the
    Host
Of Heav'n, worshipping, the Judge descends :
Consummate Triumph. Hark ! the Trumpet
    sounds,
The Breath of Michael blows the Amazing
    blast ;
The Dead arise, the Living all are Chang'd,
And Adam's family appear before Him—
Amid that throng—in that Assembly vast,
Must thou my soul appear and there receive
A Plaudit glorious or Silence sad :
Sink deep in Thought, Oh, deeper, deeper
    still :
May it ne'er be forgotten, on my Couch

Be it my dreaming subject, when awake,
Oh ! be it still remembered : for its worth
What tongue can speak, or any language
    tell ?
Then from this hour deep on my heart
    engraved
Be all my duty needful ; Ha ! that blaze
That Shock tremendous that appals me thus
Says I am not prepar'd—but I submit ;
No more will I rebel against thy sway
Nor dispute thy dominion Gracious God !
My sins shall suffer and by Grace divine
I will forsake them all and trust alone
For true felicity, for pleasure high
To Thee : who only can true pleasure give.
The Storm abates—less too the Thunder
    roars,
The Vault of Heav'n grows brighter, and the
    Sun
Strives to Emerge from yonder dusky Cloud,
More faint the flashes grow—and distant fly,
Nature resumes her charms, and from the
    Grove
Musick again is heard : the Warblers there
Attempt a feeble strain : the Dog Star now

Throws his warm beams around the weeping
    Scene ;
Salubrious Zephyrs gently fan the Air :
Love, Life, and Joy return by due degrees
And Harmony once more revisits Earth.

Heu! Quam Remotus.[1]

This poem owes its pathetic interest partly to its evident reference to Theodora—"and thee forsook." The translation is by a friend—Mr. Alfred Gough. It has appeared only in my "Life of William Cowper."

HEU ! quam remotus vescor omnibus
  Quibus fruebar sub lare patrio,
Quam nescius jucunda quondam
  Arva, domum, socios, reliqui !

Et praeter omnes te mihi flebilem,
  Te chariorem luce vel artubus,
Te vinculo nostram jugali
  Deserui tremulam sub ense

[1] This poem is appended to the copy of Cowper's Autobiography, published in 1835 by Mr. W. White, of Bedford. The original and the lines beginning "Hatred and Vengeance" were written on the same sheet of paper, which was for a long time in the possession of Mr. Isaac Handscomb, of Newport Pagnell.

Sed nec ferocem me genuit pater,
   Nec vagientem nutriit ubere
Leaena dumoso sub antro,
   Fata sed hoc voluere nostra.

Et, fluctuosum ceu mare volvitur,
   Dum commovebar mille timoribus,
Coactus in fauces Averni
   Totus atro perii sub amne.

Translation.

Far from my natal roof I sigh,
   Of all its joys, alas! bereft,
Since long ago, so thoughtlessly,
   Sweet fields and home and friends I left ;

And thee forsook, for whom mine eyes
   Weep sore, more loved than limb or life,
And linked to me by closest ties,
   A victim trembling 'neath the knife.

Yet no fierce monster was I born,
   No lioness e'er nourished me,
In some rude cave o'erhung with thorn ;
   No !—this is Destiny's decree.

My soul by countless terrors riven,
   And like the stormy ocean tossed,
Into Avernus' jaws was driven,
   In its black stream for ever lost.

ADMIRAL KEPPEL.

On the Trial of Admiral Keppel.

(END OF 1778.)

After a battle fought with the French off Brest, Keppel, who probably did not make the most of his opportunities, was court-martialled, but had the good fortune to be acquitted. Cowper, who, in common with a very large number in England, sympathised with the admiral, composed on the occasion the following lines :—

KEPPEL, returning from afar
    With laurels on his brow,
Comes home to wage a sharper war,
    And with a fiercer foe.

The blow was raised with cruel aim,
    And meant to pierce his heart,
But lighting on his well-earned fame
    Struck an immortal part.

Slander and Envy strive to tear
   His wreath so justly won,
But Truth, who made his cause her care,
   Has bound it faster on.

The charge that was design'd to sound
   The signal of disgrace,
Has only called a navy round
   To praise him to his face.

This and the following poem have appeared only in
The Universal Review.

SIR HUGH PALLISER.

An Address to the Mob on Occasion of the late Riot at the House of Sir Hugh Palliser.

(END OF 1788.)

This poem is a fellow to the preceding. Sir Hugh Palliser, the second in command of the fleet under Keppel had disobeyed the orders of his chief ; but being court-martialled, he, too, was acquitted. The mob however forced their way into his house and demolished everything—an action which aroused Cowper's indignation—hence the following :—

AND is it thus, ye base and blind,
    And fickle as the shifting wind,
Ye treat a warrior staunch and true,
Grown old in combating for you ?

Can one false step and made in haste
Thus cancel every service past ?
And have ye all at once forgot
(As whose deservings have ye not ?)
That Palliser, like Keppel brave,
Has baffled France on yonder wave ;
And when his country asked the stake
Has pledged his life for England's sake !
Though now he sink, oppressed with shame,
Forgetful of his former fame,
Yet Keppel with deserv'd applause
Proclaims him bold in Britain's cause,
And to his well-known courage pays
The tribute of heroic praise—
Go learn of him, whom ye adore,
Whose name now sets you in a roar,
Whom ye were more than half prepar'd
To pay with just the same reward,
To render praise where praise is due,
To keep his former deeds in view
Who fought and would have died for you.

The Bee and the Pineapple.

(PROBABLY SEPTEMBER, 1779.)

A BEE, allured by the perfume
  Of a rich pineapple in bloom,
Found it within a frame enclosed,
And licked the glass that interposed.
Blossoms of apricot and peach,
The flowers that blowed within his reach,
Were arrant drugs compared with that
He strove so vainly to get at
No rose could yield so rare a treat,
Nor jessamine were half so sweet.
 The gard'ner saw this much-ado
(The gardener was the master too),
And thus he said : " Poor restless bee !

I learn philosophy from thee.
I learn how just it is and wise,
To use what Providence supplies,
To leave fine titles, lordships, graces,
Rich pensions, dignities, and places—
Those gifts of a superior kind—
To those for whom they were designed.
I learn that comfort dwells alone
In that which Heaven has made our own,
That fools incur no greater pain
Than pleasure coveted in vain."

A little later, Cowper wrote another poem on the same subject—the lines which appear in every edition of Cowper with the title of "The Pineapple and the Bee." In the Ash Collection it is called—

Another on the Same.

This poem, which is the well-known version, accompanied a letter to Hill, dated October, 1779.

THE pineapples, in triple row,
    Were basking hot, and all in blow.
A bee of most deserving taste
Perceived the fragrance as he passed,
On eager wing the spoiler came,
And searched for crannies in the frame,
Urged his attempt on every side,
To every pane his trunk applied ;
But still in vain, the frame was tight,
And only pervious to the light :
Thus having wasted half the day,
He trimmed his flight another way.

Methinks, I said, in thee I find
The sin and madness of mankind.
To joys forbidden man aspires,
Consumes his soul with vain desires ;
Folly the spring of his pursuit,
And disappointment all the fruit.
While Cynthio ogles, as she passes,
The nymph between two chariot glasses,
She is the pineapple, and he
The silly unsuccessful bee.
The maid who views with pensive air
The showglass fraught with glittering ware,
Sees watches, bracelets, rings, and lockets,
But sighs at thought of empty pockets ;
Like thine, her appetite is keen,
But ah, the cruel glass between !
    Our dear delights are often such,
Exposed to view, but not to touch ;
The sight our foolish heart inflames,
We long for pineapples in frames ;
With hopeless wish one looks and lingers ;
One breaks the glass, and cuts his fingers ;
But they whom Truth and Wisdom lead,
Can gather honey from the weed.

Anti-thelyphthora, or The Doves.[1]

(JUNE 5, 1780.)

ACCOMPANYING A LETTER TO MRS. NEWTON.

In the Ash Collection this is entitled "Antithelyph-
thora," and runs as follows :—

M USE, mark the much lamented day,
    When like a Tempest feared,
First issuing on the last of May
"Thelyphthora" appeared.

That fatal eve I wandered late
    And heard the voice of love ;
The turtle thus address'd her mate,
    And soothed the listening dove :

---

[1] "Thelyphthora ; or a Treatise on Marriage," was
a work, advocating Polygamy, written by the Rev.
Martin Madan, Cowper's cousin. It created a sensa-
tion in the religious world, and provoked Cowper to
write, besides the above, a long poem entitled, "Anti-
thelyphthora," also "Love Abused," and several epi-
grams—the best of which is "If John marries Mary."

" Our mutual bond of faith and truth
 No time shall disengage,
Those blessings of our early youth
 Shall cheer our latest age :

" While innocence without disguise,
 And constancy sincere,
Shall fill the circles of those eyes,
 And mine can read them there :

" Those ills, that wait on all below,
 Shall ne'er be left by me,
Or gently felt, and only so,
 As being shared by thee.

" When lightnings flash among the trees,
 Or kites are hovering near,
I fear lest thee alone they seize,
 And know no other fear.

" 'Tis then I feel myself a wife,
 And press thy wedded side,
Resolved a union form'd for life
 Death never shall divide.

"But oh ! if fickle and unchaste
  (Forgive a transient thought),
Thou could'st become unkind at last,
  And scorn thy present lot,

"No need of lightnings from on high,
  Or kites with cruel beak ;
Denied the endearments of thine eye,
  This widow'd heart would break."

Thus sang the sweet sequester'd bird,
  Soft as the passing wind,
And I recorded what I heard,
  A lesson for mankind.

The poem as published began thus :—

Reasoning at every step he treads,
  Man yet mistakes his way,
While meaner things, whom instinct leads,
  Are rarely known to stray.

One silent eve I wander'd late,
  &c.

Tom Raban.[1]

(AUGUST 31, 1780.)

THE curate[2] and churchwarden,[3]
And eke exciseman[4] too,
Have treated poor Tom Raban
As if he was a Jew.

[1] Thomas Raban, the carpenter-parson of Olney, and one of the leading characters of Cowper's Letters, was born in 1734 at Turvey, and became a hearer of the Rev. Moses Browne and the Rev. John Newton. With Newton's successors Mr. Raban could not get on. He wanted to be used, and they had not the gumption to use him. So—the old, old tale—John Wesley in little—he turned Nonconformist, and became one of the leading pillars of Independency in North Bucks. Though he had the care of an Independent church at Yardley Hastings, he still worked as a carpenter at Olney. He died May 13, 1802, and was buried in Olney churchyard, his funeral sermon being preached in the market-place, by the Rev. William Bull, the concourse being too great for the meeting-house. His biography has been written.

[2] Rev. Mr. Page, Newton's successor at Olney.

[3] Mr. Maurice Smith.   [4] Mr. Tolson.

For they have sent him packing,
   No more in church to work,
Whatever may be lacking ;
   As if he was a Turk.

Thus carry they the farce on,
   Which is great cause of grief,
Until that Page, the parson,
   Turn over a new leaf.

Thus says the muse, and though her fav'rite
  cue
Is fiction, yet her song is sometimes true.

The Cancelled Passage in Expostulation.

(FEBRUARY, 1781.)

" HAST thou admitted, with a blind, fond
trust,
The lie that burned my father's bones to
dust,
That first adjudged them heretics, then
sent
Their souls to heaven and cursed them as
they went ?
The lie that Scripture strips of its disguise,
And execrates above all other lies,
The lie that claps a lock on mercy's plan,
And gives the key to yon infirm old man,
Who once ensconced in apostolic chair
Is deified, and sits omniscient there ;

The lie that knows no kindred, owns no
    friend
But him that makes its progress his chief
    end,
That having spilt much blood, makes that a
    boast,
And canonizes him that sheds the most ?
Away with charity that soothes a lie,
And thrusts the truth with scorn and anger
    by ;
Shame on the candour and the gracious
    smile
Bestowed on them that light the martyr's
    pile,
While insolent disdain in frowns expressed
Attends the tenets that endured the test !
Grant them rights of men, and while they
    cease
To vex the peace of others grant them peace :
But trusting bigots whose false zeal has
    made
Treachery their duty, thou art self-betrayed."

    The above passage was actually set up, but only
a few copies were struck off. It was, no doubt,

cancelled for fear of wounding the feelings of Cowper's esteemed Roman Catholic friends, the Throckmortons, and Cowper, "working like a tailor who sews a patch upon a hole in a coat," made twenty-four lines to fill the gap—"Hast thou, when Heaven . . . by renewed offence."

The Degeneracy of the Clergy.

WRITTEN ON A LACE-BUYER'S BILL. (POSSIBLY EXCISED FROM THE " PROGRESS OF ERROR.")

METHINKS I see thee decently arrayed
 In long-flowed nightgown of stuff
  damask made,
Thy cassock underneath it closely braced
With surcingle about thy moderate waist.
Thy morning wig, grown tawny to the view,
Though once a grizzle, and thy square-toed
  shoe.
The day was when the sacerdotal race
Esteemed their proper habit no disgrace,
Or rather when the garb their order wears
Was not disgraced as now by being theirs.

The Joy of the Cross.

(AUGUST, 1782.)

Translated from Madam Guion. The following, which is from the Ash Collection, differs considerably from the accepted version.

LONG plunged in sorrow, I resign
  My soul to that dear hand of Thine,
    Without reserve or fear ;
That hand shall wipe my streaming eyes ;
Or into smiles of glad surprise
    Transform the falling tear.

My sole possession is Thy love ;
In earth beneath, or heaven above,
    I have no other store ;
And, though with fervent suit I pray,
And importune Thee night and day,
    I ask Thee nothing more.

Obedient to Thy law's sweet force
My rapid hours pursue their course
   And I Thy sovereign will,
Without a wish to escape my doom,
Though still a sufferer from the womb,
   And doomed to suffer still.

By Thy command, where'er I stray,
Sorrow attends me all my way,
   A never-failing friend ;
And, if my sufferings may augment
Thy praise, behold me well content—
   Let sorrow still attend !

It cost me no regret, that she,
Who followed Christ, should follow me.
   And though, where'er she goes,
Thorns spring spontaneous at her feet,
I love her, and extract a sweet
   From all my bitter woes.

Adieu ! ye vain delights of earth,
Insipid sports, and childish mirth,
   I taste no sweets in you ;
Unknown delights are in the cross,
All joy beside to me is dross ;
   And Jesus thought so too.

The cross ! Oh, ravishment and bliss—
How grateful e'en its anguish is :
   Its bitterness how sweet !
There every sense, and all the mind,
In all her faculties refined,
   Tastes happiness complete.

Souls once enabled to disdain
Base sublunary joys, maintain
   Their dignity secure ;
The fever of desire is pass'd,
And love has all its genuine taste,
   Is delicate and pure.

Self-love no grace in sorrow sees,
Consults her own peculiar ease :
   'Tis all the bliss she knows :
But nobler aims true Love employ ;
In self-denial is her joy,
   In suffering her repose.

Sorrow and love go side by side :
Nor height nor depth can e'er divide
   Their heaven-appointed bands :
Those dear associates still are one,
Nor till the race of life is run
   Disjoin their wedded hands.

Jesus, avenger of our fall,
Thou faithful lover, above all
   The cross has ever borne !
Oh, tell me—life is in Thy voice—
How much afflictions were Thy choice,
   And sloth and ease Thy scorn !

Thy choice and mine shall be the same,
Inspirer of that deathless flame
   Which Thou inspirst alone.
To take the cross and follow Thee
Where love and duty lead, shall be
   My pleasure and my crown.

My rapid hours pursue the course
Prescribed them by love's sweetest force,
   And I Thy sovereign will,
Without a wish to escape my doom ;
Though still a sufferer from the womb,
   And doom'd to suffer still.

Thy choice and mine shall be the same,
Inspirer of that holy flame
   Which must for ever blaze,
To take the cross and follow Thee
Where love and duty lead, shall be
   My portion and my praise.

The Love of God the End of Life.

(AUGUST, 1782.)

Translated from Madam Guion (Ash Collection).
Differing considerably from the accepted version.

SINCE we must sorrow and why not?
  For me I wish no gentler lot,
But meekly wait my last remove,
Seeking only growth in love.

No bliss I seek, but to fulfil
In life, in death, Thy lovely will;
No succours in my woes I want,
Save what Thou art pleased to grant.

Our days are numbered, let us spare
Our anxious hearts a needless care ;
'Tis Thine to number out our days ;
Ours to give them to Thy praise.

Love is our only business here,
Love simple, constant, and sincere,
O blessed days Thy servants see
Spent, O Lord ! in pleasing Thee.

Against Interested Love.

Written on the back of the translation from
Madame Guion—

"Blest, who far from all mankind."

(PROBABLY 1782.)

WHO does not blush when charged with
    selfish views
Man boasts for man a principle of love ;
But each with God a different course pursues,
And interest is the spring by which they
    move.
Oh, blindness of our mean and stupid race !
The selfish and the sordid we despise,

And yet the love of God incurs disgrace,
While love to man is sounded to the skies.
How speaks the world ?—in Friendship's
    sacred cause
A generous service is its own reward,
A maxim all have stamped with their ap-
    plause,
How speaks the world ? My dear and
    valued friend
My recompense is found in serving you.

To a Young Lady who Stole a Pen from the Prince of Wales's Standish.

SWEET nymph, who art, it seems, accused
  Of stealing George's pen,
Use it thyself, and having used,
  E'en give it him again.

The plume of his that has one scrap
  Of thy good sense expressed
Will be a feather in his cap
  Worth more than all his crest.

LADY AUSTEN.

(From a miniature in possession of Dr. GRINDON of Olney.)

To a Lady (Lady Austen)

WHO WORE A LOCK OF HIS HAIR SET WITH
DIAMONDS.

(ABOUT 1784.)

THE star that beams on Anna's breast
    Conceals her William's hair ;
'Twas lately severed from the rest
    To be promoted there.

The heart that beats beneath that breast
    Is William's well I know,
A nobler prize and richer far
    Than India could bestow.

She thus his favoured lock prefers
To make her William shine ;
The ornament indeed is hers,
But all the honour mine.

The above lines reached Mr. John Bruce and the Rev. Canon Benham from different sources. They were first printed, I believe, in Messrs. Macmillan's Globe edition of Cowper (1870), but copies of them had long been in the hands of students.

MISS ANN GREEN.

To a Young Lady (Miss Ann Green).

WITH A PRESENT OF TWO COXCOMBS.

(PERHAPS ABOUT 1784.)

TWO powdered Coxcombs [1] wait at your command,
And what is strange, both dressed by Nature's hand,
Like other fops they dread a sudden shower
And seek a shelter in your closest bower,
Showy like them, like them they yield no fruit,
But then to make amends they both are mute.

The above was given to me by Mrs. A. Hipwell, of Olney, who had had it in her possession many years. The lines which appear in the Globe edition of

---

[1] Cockscombs — flowers, of course. Cowper is punning.

Cowper (Macmillan) were obtained by Canon Benham from another source and differ from the above, which is the better version, in the first, third, and fourth lines. Miss Green, to whom the Cockscombs were given, was Lady Austen's niece. She married, May 26, 1791, Dr. Grindon, Cowper's physician, grandfather of the present Dr. Grindon, of Olney. Her mother, Martha Richardson (the lady referred to in the poem beginning, " Dear Anna, between friend and friend ") was married first to Mr. Green, a brewer, of Chelsea, and afterwards to the Rev. Thomas Jones, curate of Clifton Reynes, near Olney.

The Critics Chastised.

WRITTEN ON A PAGE OF "THE MONTHLY REVIEW."

(1784.)

THESE critics, who to faith no quarter
    grant,
But call it mere hypocrisy and cant [1]
To make a just acknowledgment of praise,
And thanks to God for governing our ways,

---

[1] The Reviewer had stigmatised the opinions of the Rev. John Newton as "cant."

Approve Confucius more, and Zoroaster,
Than Christ's own servant, or that servant's
    Master.

For the above we are indebted to an anonymous
correspondent of the *Record*, Feb. 20, 1867.   Their
genuineness is beyond doubt.

Box and Bays.

(FEB. 2, 1791.)

With the little folks at Weston Hall Cowper made himself very agreeable. He let them run him up and down the long corridors in a chair on wheels and played "spillikins" and other games with them. Little Tom Gifford, who did not always pronounce the poet's name properly—an ailment, by the by, with which older folks than he have been afflicted—used to call him Mr. Toot, and in several of his letters Cowper signs himself "W. Toot." One day (Feb. 2, 1791) Tom gave Lady Hesketh a sprig of box, "desiring her in his way to give it to Toot as a present from himself, on which occasion Toot, seized with a fit of poetic enthusiasm, said or seemed to say :

DEAR TOM! my muse this moment sounds your praise,
And turns at once your sprig of box to bays."

Yardley Oak.

(1791.)

With the excised passages restored and the principal
alterations made by Cowper pointed out. The excised
passages are in brackets, the rejected words appear as
footnotes. The manuscript is preserved in the Cowper
Museum at Olney, to which it was presented by
H. W. Collingridge, Esq., on the Centenary of Cowper's death, 25th April, 1900.

SURVIVOR sole, and hardly such, of all
   That once lived here, thy brethren, at
      my birth,
(Since which I number threescore winters
      past,)
A shattered veteran, hollow-trunk'd perhaps,
As now, and with excoriate forks deform,

YARDLEY OAK.

(Photograph by THE GRAPHOTONE COMPANY.)

Relics of ages ! Could a mind, imbued
With truth [1] from Heaven, created thing
  adore,
I might with reverence kneel, and worship
  thee.
  It seems idolatry, with some excuse,
When our forefather Druids in their oaks
Imagined sanctity. The conscience, yet
Unpurified by an authentic act
Of amnesty, the meed of blood divine,
Loved not the light, but, gloomy, into gloom
Of thickest shades, like Adam after taste
Of fruit proscribed, as to a refuge, fled.
  Thou wast a bauble once ; a cup and ball,
Which babes might play with ; and the
  thievish jay,
Seeking her food, with ease might have pur-
  loined
The auburn nut that held thee, swallowing
  down
Thy yet close-folded latitude of boughs
And all thine embryo vastness at a gulp.
But Fate thy growth decreed ; autumnal
  rains

[1] Milk.

Beneath thy parent tree mellowed the soil
Designed thy cradle ; and a skipping deer,
With pointed hoof dibbling the glebe, pre-
    pared
The soft receptacle, in which, secure,
Thy rudiments should sleep the winter
    through.
    So Fancy dreams.   Disprove it, if ye can,[1]
Ye reasoners[2] broad awake, whose busy
    search
Of argument, employed too oft amiss,
Sifts half the pleasures of short life away !
    Thou fell'st mature ; and in the loamy
    clod[3]
Swelling[4] with vegetative force instinct
Didst burst thine egg, as theirs the fabled
    Twins,
Now stars ; two lobes, protruding, pair'd
    exact ;
A leaf succeeded, and another leaf,
And, all the elements thy puny growth
Fostering propitious, thou becamest a twig.

---

[1] If thou canst.   [2] Thou reasoner.
[3] Nurturing clod.   [4] Reposed.

Who lived when thou wast such ? Oh,
     couldst thou speak,
As in Dodona once thy kindred trees
Oracular, I would not curious ask
The future, best unknown, but at thy mouth
Inquisitive, the less ambiguous past.
   By thee I might correct, erroneous oft,
The clock of history, facts and events
Timing more punctual, unrecorded facts
Recovering, and misstated setting aright——
Desperate attempt, till trees shall speak
     again !
   Time made thee what thou wast, king of
     the woods ;
And time hath made thee what thou art—a
     cave
For owls to roost in. Once thy spreading
     boughs
O'erhung the champaign ; and the numerous
     flocks
That grazed it, stood beneath that ample
     cope [1]
Uncrowded, yet safe shelter'd from the
     storm.

[1] That ample cope beneath.

No flock frequents thee now.   Thou hast
    outlived
Thy popularity and art become
(Unless verse rescue thee awhile) a thing
Forgotten, as the foliage of thy youth.
    While thus through all the stages thou hast
        push'd [1]
Of treeship—first a seedling hid in grass ;
Then twig ; then sapling ; and, as century
    roll'd
Slow after century, a giant bulk
Of girth enormous, with moss cushioned root [2]
Upheaved above the soil, and sides emboss'd
With prominent wens globose,—till at the
    last
The rottenness, which Time is charged to
    inflict
On other mighty ones, found also thee.
    What exhibitions various hath the world
Witness'd of mutability in all

[1] Moved.
[2] [Of full grown timber with moss-cushioned root
    High-swoln above the soil, and sides embossed
    With wens protub'rant, till at last the curse
    That finds out all the great ones of the earth—
    The curse of rottenness—found also thee.]

That we account most durable below!
Change is the diet, on which all subsist,
Created changeable, and change at last
Destroys them.   Skies uncertain now the heat
Transmitting cloudless, and the solar beam[1]
Now quenching in a boundless sea of
   clouds,—
Calm and alternate storm, moisture and
   drought,
Invigorate by turns the springs of life[2]
In all that live, plant, animal, and man,
And in conclusion mar them.   Nature's
   threads,
Fine passing thought, e'en in their coarsest
   works,
Delight in agitation, yet sustain
The force, that agitates not unimpair'd ;
But, worn by frequent impulse, to the cause
Of their best tone their dissolution owe.
   Thought cannot spend[3] itself, comparing
      still

[1] Intercepting now.
[2] Between this line and the next, "All-binding
frost and all unbinding thaw."
[3] Tire.

The great and little of thy lot, thy growth
From almost nullity into a state
Of matchless grandeur, and declension thence,
Slow, into such magnificent decay.
Time was when, settling on thy leaf, a fly
Could shake thee to the root—and time has
    been
When tempests could not.   At thy firmest
    age [1]
Thou hadst within thy bole solid contents,
That might have ribb'd the sides and plank'd
    the deck
Of some flagged admiral ; and tortuous arms,
The shipwright's darling treasure, didst
    present
To the four-quartered winds, robust and bold,
Warp'd into tough knee-timber, many a load !
But the axe spared thee.   In those thriftier
    days
Oaks fell not, hewn by thousands, to supply
The bottomless demands of contest, waged
For senatorial honours.   Thus to Time
The task was left to whittle thee away
With his sly scythe, whose ever-nibbling edge,

[1] In thy prime of strength.

Noiseless, an atom and an atom more,
Disjoining [1] from the rest, has, unobserved, [2]
Achieved a labour, which had, far and wide, [3]
By man performed, made all the forest ring.
    Embowelled now, and of thy ancient self
Possessing nought but the scoop'd rind, that
        seems
A huge throat calling to the clouds for drink,
Which it would give in rivulets to thy root.
Thou temptest none, but rather much forbid'st
The feller's toil, which thou couldst ill re-
        quite.
Yet is thy root sincere, sound as the rock,
A quarry of stout spurs, and knotted fangs,
Which, crook'd into a thousand whimsies,
        clasp
The stubborn soil, and hold thee still erect. [4]
    So stands a kingdom, whose foundation yet
Fails not, in virtue and in wisdom laid.
Though all the superstructure, by the tooth
Pulverised of venality, a shell
Stands now, and semblance only of itself !

[1] Detaching.   [2] By degrees.
[3] Insensible the task performed as seen.
[4] Secure.

Thine arms have left thee. Winds have
    rent them off
Long since, and rovers of the forest wild
With bow and shaft have burnt them. Some
    have left
A splinter'd stump bleached to a snowy white ;
And some memorial none [1] where once they
    grew.
Yet life still lingers in thee, and puts forth
Proof not contemptible of what she can,
Even where death predominates. The
    spring
Finds thee not less alive to her sweet force
Than yonder upstarts of the neighbouring
    wood,
So much thy juniors, who their birth received
Half a millennium since the date of thine.
    But since, although well qualified by age
To teach, no spirit dwells in thee, nor voice
May be expected from thee, seated here
On thy distorted root, with hearers none,
Or prompter, save the scene, I will perform [2]
Myself the oracle, and will discourse

    [1] No trace or sign.   [2] Become.

In my own ear such matter as I may.
[Thou, like myself, hast stage by stage
    attained
Life's wintry bourn ; thou, after many years,
I after few ; but few or many prove
A span in retrospect ; for I can touch
With my least finger's end my own decease
And with extended thumb my natal hour,
And hadst thou also skill in measurement
As I, the past would seem as short to thee.
Evil and few—said Jacob—at an age
Thrice mine, and few and evil, I may think
The Prediluvian race, whose buxom youth
Endured two centuries, accounted theirs.
" Shortlived as foliage is the race of man.
The wind shakes down the leaves, the bud
    ding grove
Soon teems with others, and in spring they
    grow.
So pass mankind. One generation meets
Its destined period, and a new succeeds."
Such was the tender but undue complaint
Of the Mæonian in old time ; for who
Would drawl out centuries in tedious strife
Severe with mental and corporeal ill

And would not rather choose a shorter race
To glory, a few decads here below ? [1]]
    One man alone, the father of us all,
Drew not his life from woman ; never gazed,
With mute unconsciousness of what he saw,
On all around him ; learned not by degrees,
Nor owed articulation to his ear ;
But, moulded by his Maker into man,
At once, upstood [2] intelligent, surveyed
All creatures, with precision, understood
Their purport, uses, properties, assign'd
To each his name significant, and, filled
With love and wisdom, rendered back to
      Heaven
In praise harmonious the first air he drew.
He was excused the penalties of dull [3]

    [1] Footnote in Cowper's handwriting : "The lines marked with inverted commas are borrowed from my own Translation of Homer. Iliad 6, line 175."
    [2] With look.
    [3] The six last lines about Adam were at first written thus :—

[He was excused the penalties of dull
Minority ; no primer with his thumb
He soiled, no grammar with his tears, but rose
Accomplished in the only tongue on earth
Taught then, the tongue in which he spake with God.]

Minority. No tutor charged his hand
With the thought-tracing quill, or task'd his
    mind
With problems.   History, not wanted yet,
Leaned on her elbow, watching Time, whose
    course,
Eventful, should supply her with a theme, . . .

To Sir John Fenn.

(The first editor of the Paston Letters.)

(May 20, 1792.)

TWO omens seem [1] propitious to my fame,
    Your spouse embalms my verse and you
        my name,
A name which, all self-flatt'ry far apart,
Belongs to one who venerates in his heart
The wise and good, and therefore of the few
Known by those titles,[2] Sir, both yours and
    you.

It is unknown to what incident the above refers.
The lines were sent to "Johnny of Norfolk" in a letter
dated May 20, 1792. Mr. Johnson at once forwarded
them to Sir John.

[1] First written, "Two signs appear."
[2] First written, "Distinguished claimants."

To Mary.

(AUTUMN OF 1793.)

From what is probably the last original copy—that presented to the Cowper Museum, Olney, by E. P. Ash, Esq. It contains an additional stanza, marked here with an asterisk, and "the" instead of "thy" in Stanza Nine.

THE twentieth year is well nigh past
    Since first our sky was overcast ;—
Ah would that this might be the last !
                    My Mary !

Thy spirits have a fainter flow,
I see thee daily weaker grow :—
'Twas my distress that brought thee low,
                    My Mary !

Thy needles, once a shining store,
For my sake restless heretofore,
Now rust disused, and shine no more,
                              My Mary ! [1]

For though thou gladly wouldst fulfil
The same kind office for me still,
Thy sight now seconds not thy will,
                              My Mary !

But well thou play'dst the housewife's part.
And all thy threads with magic art
Have wound themselves about this heart,
                              My Mary !

[1] Stanzas Three and Four originally ran as follows :—

> Thy needles, once a shining store,
> Discernible by thee no more,
> Rust in disuse, their service o'er,
>   My Mary !
>
> But thy ingenious work remains,
> Nor small the profit it obtains
> Since thou esteemst my pleasure gains
>   My Mary !

Thy indistinct expressions seem
Like language uttered in a dream :
Yet me they charm, whate'er the theme,
     My Mary !

Thy silver locks, once auburn bright,
Are still more lovely in my sight
Than golden beams of orient light,
     My Mary !

For could I view nor them nor thee,
What sight worth seeing could I see ?
The sun would rise in vain for me,
     My Mary !

Partakers of the sad decline,
Thy hands their little force resign ;
Yet gently pressed, press gently mine,
     My Mary !

* And then I feel that still I hold
A richer store ten thousandfold
Than misers' fancy in their gold,
     My Mary !

Such feebleness of limbs thou provest,
That now at every step thou movest,
Upheld by two ; yet still thou lovest,

                              My Mary !

And still to love, though press'd with ill,
In wintry age to feel no chill,
With me is to be lovely still,

                              My Mary !

But ah ! by constant heed I know,
How oft the sadness that I show
Transforms thy smiles to looks of woe,

                              My Mary !

And should my future lot be cast
With much resemblance of the past,
Thy worn-out heart will break at last,

                              My Mary !

Morsels.

DEVOID OF LITERARY MERIT.

Given merely to illustrate Cowper's droll habit of dropping at all times and on any occasion into playful rhyme.

THE MUSLIN IS FOUND.

(At the end of a letter to Unwin, June 8, 1783.)

THE muslin is found, the gown is admired,
    Procure us some franks—adieu, I am
        tired.

THE HAMPER.

Cowper had just received a hamper, so, writing to Lady Hesketh, June 23, 1791, he bursts out into thanks as follows :—

WE have received beef, tongues, and tea,
And certainly from none but thee ;
Therefore with all our power of lungs,
Thanks for beef, and tea, and tongues.

HAYLEY'S PORTRAIT.

(NOVEMBER 25, 1792.)

Cowper was expecting Hayley's portrait. In a letter
to Hayley he says :—

ACHILLES and Hector and Homer and all
When your face appears shall come down
from the wall,
And mine, theme of many an angry remark,
Shall then hide its pickpocket looks in the
dark.

AN EPIGRAM.

At the end of a letter to Lady Hesketh (March, 1793),
preserved in the Cowper Museum at Olney.

AN epigram is but a feeble thing
With straw in tale, stuck there by way of
sting.

WESTON LODGE

(Cowper's House, Weston Underwood).

www.ingramcontent.com/pod-product-compliance
Lightning Source LLC
Chambersburg PA
CBHW020035030726
47499CB00007B/2436